COP 8

E
Hodges
FREE AS A FROG

DATE DUE

JAN 19 71 DELANO		
NOV 20 79 BELRIDGE		
APR 15 80 McFARLAND		
ARVIN SEP 24 '81		

Honoring my Goddaughter and Niece,
Ann Denny Solodar

FREE AS A FROG

Free as a Frog

BY ELIZABETH JAMISON HODGES

DRAWINGS BY PAUL GIOVANOPOULOS

 ADDISON-WESLEY

**An Addisonian Press Book**

The Addison-Wesley Publishing Company, Inc.
Reading, Massachusetts
Library of Congress catalog card number 73–88687
Printed in the United States of America
First Printing
Single Edition (Reinforced)

John Frederick Allen was six years old but still small enough to sit under a table while he watched his sister dance.

Vinnie's brown legs flashed in the sunlight coming through a window. Inside him Johnnie could feel the music bouncing all around.

It was cozy and safe under the table. He was in a little house all his own, and no one seemed to notice him.

The music stopped. Several pairs of hands were clapping.
Some neighbors were there, but Johnnie could tell Mother's
clap. It was soft like her voice. And Daddy's clap had a
large warm sound.

Daddy said, "That's great Vinnie, but why dance so hard?"
"I like to," she said. "Makes me feel like a bird."
She stretched out her arms.
"Free as a bird," she said with a little leap as if she were flying.

Mother said, "It makes us happy just to watch you."
Johnnie wished he could do something to make everyone
happy and have them clap, but he dared not try. Vinnie
was ten years old and seemed to do everything better
than he could.

Especially, Johnnie wished he could talk easily as she did.
People sometimes made fun of him when he spoke.
Hiding under the table he could think about things.

"F-F-Free as a b-bird," Johnnie said softly to himself.
He liked the way the word "Free" felt and repeated it. It
began with his upper front teeth pressed against his lower
lip. Then he opened his mouth wider and let his breath
go spilling out.

In school next day, when "Share and Tell" began, Johnnie
scrunched down in his seat. He had nothing to share,
and the idea of telling made him feel a sort of chill inside.
Sometimes, he was even embarrassed for others when
they talked in front of the class.

He looked around. Miss Derry called on Tom, who had
been waving his arm.
Tom stood up with an important look on his face. He
showed the class a very small camera.
"Friend of my father's sent me this from Tokyo," Tom said.
Miss Derry asked him to show where Tokyo was on a
map at the front of the room.
Tom used the pointer.
"Right here in Japan," he said.

At recess it seemed that everyone wanted to have a close look at the camera. Tom showed how it worked. Then he took a picture of some classmates. From a distance, Johnnie watched them smile.

After school as he walked along, Johnnie thought to himself, I wish, I *wish* I had something everyone would think is really great. When he reached home, he made himself a peanut butter sandwich, and waited impatiently for his mother to return from work.

When she did, Johnnie said, "Has D-D-Daddy a f-friend in Tokyo?"
"I don't think so," Mother said, sitting down at the kitchen table. "Why?"
Johnnie put his head in her lap. It was hard to explain.

"Tokyo's a long way off,"
she said. "Daddy's friends
live around here where he can
see them often."
Johnnie went outdoors and
down the sidewalk a short
distance till he came to the park.
Some tall trees were there, and
a pond. Johnnie walked slowly
through the grass until he was
near the water.

Suddenly he saw a small frog. It was squatting on some sandy ground beside the pond. Shiny and green, with very bright eyes, it hopped near Johnnie's foot.

He leaned over and picked the frog up. It felt wet and slippery in Johnnie's hands. With one finger he found something moving back and forth inside the frog's throat. It felt like a little ball.

Johnnie looked around and saw a trash barrel on the sidewalk. Sticking out of it was a jar. It was empty and looked clean. Very gently he placed the frog in the jar.
I'll call him "Hoppy," Johnnie thought, as he put some water, grass, and a little earth in the jar. Then, with a sharp stone, he made an opening in the top of the jar to let in air.

Next day when it was time for "Share and Tell," Johnnie took a deep breath and raised a hand.
Miss Derry looked pleased.
"Johnnie, what do you have to share with us?" she said.
"Hoppy," Johnnie said.
Then he could hardly believe how great it was. Everyone crowded around asking to see Hoppy. Miss Derry even told them to go back to their seats or they might smother the little frog.
At recess it was even better.
"Let me see him first," said one.
"No, me," said another.
And Tom asked if he could hold Hoppy.

On the way home Johnnie
thought, I am happier than ever
before in my life. He even felt
sort of light as if he had balloons
inside of him. He had Hoppy
and he had shown him to the
class.

The happy balloon feeling lasted until after supper that same day. Then Johnnie looked at Hoppy and saw that something was wrong.

He was not jumping. He was hardly moving at all.

"Eat s-some g-g-grass," Johnnie said.

"Maybe he eats something else," Vinnie said.

"Maybe he doesn't like being in a jar," Mother said. "Maybe he wants to be free and swim in the pond."

Inside Johnnie the balloon feeling had suddenly gone. Instead, he felt tight and heavy. He wanted to take the frog to school every day, but Hoppy was very still. He even seemed to have trouble breathing.

Johnnie carried Hoppy slowly along the street and back to the edge of the pond. There Johnnie took the little frog out of the jar and put him on the ground near the water. For a moment Hoppy remained very still, just where Johnnie had put him. Then as a mosquito flew too close, the frog raised his head. His tongue darted out and back. Suddenly, with legs outspread, Hoppy dove headlong into the water.

Johnnie laughed. Hoppy's dive had made him think of his sister's dancing.

"You jumped l-like Vinnie," Johnnie said, and added, "If you don't go far, maybe I'll see you again."

As Johnnie turned to leave, he felt surprised that he had said so much right out loud. Tomorrow he would tell the class how he had let Hoppy go.

When Johnnie came home, he heard some music and saw
Vinnie dancing again in the living room with her arms
outstretched. Mother was looking on, her sewing in
her lap.
For a moment, Johnnie stood and watched his sister.
Then he bent his elbows and raised his arms so they looked
a little like Hoppy's legs.
"I'm f-free as a frog," he said with a chuckle and dove head
first into the sofa cushions.

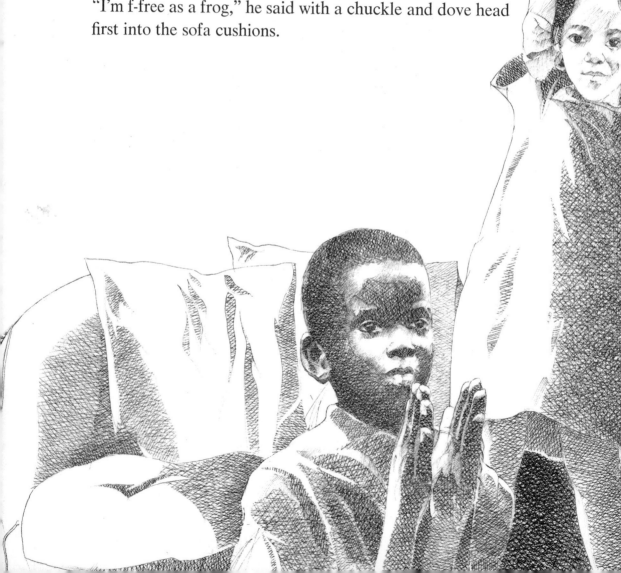

When he looked up, the happy balloon feeling had come back. Mother and Vinnie were smiling at him and clapping too.

"Free as a frog," John Frederick Allen said, laughing, and he dove into the sofa cushions again.